Curtain Going Up!

by
Debra Weiss

Watermill Press

Contents of this edition copyright © 1983 by Watermill
Press, Mahwah, New Jersey

Printed in the United States of America

Illustrations by James R. Odbert

ISBN 0-89375-818-3

Contents

What a Break!

Patty Newton pinned the number 185 onto her leotard. She looked around the dance studio, amazed. She had never before seen so many dancers in one room!

Patty turned to her friend Gail. "How many women do you think are here?" she asked.

"Let's see," Gail said. She thought for a minute. "I'd say there are about 250 women."

"I've never seen such a huge audition," Patty said. "I think we're just wasting our time."

"Maybe so. But I don't mind waiting around just to get a glimpse of Carl Matthews, the director."

"I hope he shows up," Patty added.

Just then, the famous director walked through the door. Four or five people were with him. A murmur went through the crowd. Mr. Matthews was led to a seat at the front of the room.

"I can die happy now," Gail whispered to Patty.

"He looks even better in person than he does in pictures," Patty sighed.

A woman stood up to speak. "Mr.

"I've never seen such a huge audition,"
Patty said.

Matthews would like to thank everyone for coming to this audition. Because there are so many of you, we're going to have to typecast. Please don't take it personally."

There was one bad thing about type-casting. Only appearance counted. The dancers wouldn't even get a chance to perform if they were out at this early stage.

Patty looked at Gail. "Whoever gets cut first waits by the water fountain, O.K.?" she asked.

Gail nodded and gave Patty a wink. "Good luck," she said.

"You, too!" said Patty.

The women were lined up in groups of twenty. Mr. Matthews and his assistants sat at a long table at the front of the room. The first group of women stood in front of them. Every so often,

8

Mr. Matthews whispered something to the man on his left. The man wrote down some notes.

Then the woman running the audition stood up. She called out the numbers of the dancers in the first group who were to stay. "And the rest, thank you," she added with a smile. "Numbers 181 to 200 are next," she said.

Patty and Gail had numbers 185 and 186. They took their places in line. Patty sucked in her stomach and smiled. Gail put her hands on her hips and looked Mr. Matthews right in the eye. The women in line waited anxiously. The minutes seemed like hours.

Finally, the woman announced the decision. "Numbers 181 and 190, please stay. And the rest, thank you," she said.

Patty and Gail looked at each other.

They'd been cut. They picked up their dance bags and went back to the dressing room.

"What a letdown!" Patty said.

"I know," Gail sighed. "What do you think they were looking for?"

"I'm not sure. It seemed as if they were only keeping tall blonds."

"But they asked that short, dark-haired girl to stay, too!" Gail noticed.

"Oh, who knows? Maybe we wore the wrong color leotards," Patty said with a shrug. She stuffed her leotard into her bag and looked at Gail. "What do you say we go for a cup of coffee?"

"I'd love to, but I've got to get to work," Gail replied. "Will you be in dance class tomorrow?"

"You bet."

"Me, too. See you!" Gail waved as she

headed toward the door.

"See you!" Patty called.

After Gail left, Patty went to a nearby coffee shop. She couldn't go home just yet. She needed to sort out her thoughts. She counted all the auditions she'd been to lately. She could think of at least ten in the last three weeks! And none of them had worked out.

What's wrong with me? she thought. *Is it my dancing? My singing? My looks?* She hadn't had a dance job in four months. Now she was working part-time in an office to support herself.

Patty looked at her watch. It was getting late. She paid for her coffee and walked to the subway.

When Patty reached her apartment, a delicious smell filled the air. Her roommate, Judy, was in the kitchen cooking a big pot of spaghetti sauce.

"Mmm, that smells great!" Patty said, walking into the kitchen. "Can I have a taste?"

"Sure, Patty! But watch out—it's hot!" Judy answered.

"Yum! This tastes terrific," Patty said. She took another taste. "When will it be ready?"

"It will be ready in five minutes," Judy replied. "By the way, how was the audition?"

"Don't ask," Patty groaned. She made a face.

"Well, I've got some good news for you," Judy said. "That handsome friend of yours, George Tarkas, called long distance for you. He said it was *very* important."

Patty smiled. She had met George

Patty's roommate, Judy, was in the kitchen cooking a big pot of spaghetti sauce.

last summer when they worked together in a show. George was a terrific dancer. She'd liked him a lot back then, but he already had a girlfriend. Patty had heard that they had broken up after the summer.

"Did he leave his number?" Patty asked.

"It's right there," Judy said, pointing to a small pad of paper.

Patty took the phone into the bedroom. She dialed George's number. Her heart was pounding.

"Hi, George. This is Patty Newton," she said.

"Hi, Patty. Listen, I've got an offer that I hope you won't refuse...," George began.

George was dancing in a musical comedy. The theater was about 100 miles away from the city. Last night at re-hearsal, George's partner had injured herself. They needed someone to replace her right away. "Can you do it?" he asked Patty.

"You bet I can do it!" she said.

After Patty hung up, she raced into the kitchen. She gave Judy a big hug and told her the news. She'd be gone for about six weeks—two weeks of rehear-sal and four weeks of performances.

"I'll miss you, Pat, but I'm really happy for you!" Judy said.

The next two days, Patty was busy shopping, packing, and saying good-bye to her friends. She began learning the songs from the show. Before she knew it, it was time to leave.

"I'll write to you about everything," Patty promised Judy as Patty boarded

"I'll write to you about everything,"
Patty promised Judy.

the train at the station.

"Especially George Tarkas," Judy said with a wink.

Patty waved to Judy as the train pulled out of the station. She was off!

First Rehearsal

Patty felt excited as her train neared the station. The theater was really out in the country! Rolling hills and forests stretched as far as Patty could see. In a field to the right, a girl was picking apples. She waved as the train pulled into Riverdale Junction.

In an instant, Patty spotted George

Tarkas. He was waiting for her on the platform. His thick brown hair was streaked with gold. He looked even more handsome than Patty remembered.

I'm going to like it here, she said to herself. She waved at George through the window.

As soon as she stepped off the train, George grabbed her bag. He gave her a friendly hug.

"Hey, Patty, it's great to see you! Has it really been a whole year?" George said.

"Almost," said Patty. "It's hard to believe, isn't it?"

"Well, I'm really looking forward to dancing with you again. You're a life-saver to come up here on such short notice."

"I'm glad to be here," Patty said shyly.

19

*George looked even more handsome than
Patty remembered.*

"Thanks so much for getting me this job! I needed to get away from the city for a while."

"I know what you mean about the city," George said. "It's exciting there. But it's so crazy sometimes. I've only been here two weeks, and I feel like a country boy already! The whole cast went to pick apples last weekend. Here, try one." George pulled an apple out of his pocket.

Patty laughed and put the apple in her purse. "I'll save it for later," she said. "Frankly, I'm too nervous to eat anything right now."

George stopped in front of a blue car and got out his keys.

"Is this your car?" Patty asked.

"No, it belongs to the director, Ned Laramie. Boy, will he be glad to see you!

21

He's been a wreck since Mary injured herself the other day."

Patty slid onto the front seat. "George, what happened to Mary?" she asked.

"Well, we have this romantic dance in the second act. She comes running toward me and leaps into my arms. Then I swing her around and lift her up in a high arch.

"Mary caught her heel on something while she was running toward me. She fell hard on her right side and broke her arm."

"How horrible!" Patty exclaimed.

"She took it pretty badly. After she got a cast put on her arm, she took the next train out of Riverdale. But at least you're here to help now."

As they drove toward the theater, Patty wondered what kind of man Ned

Laramie was. She had only ten days to learn Mary's role. That wasn't much time!

Soon George and Patty were driving up the tree-lined road to the theater. Suddenly, George said, "Oh, Patty, I almost forgot to tell you. Ned thinks you've done this show before. I told him that to calm him down. So just act as if you know what's going on. I'll pull you through." George smiled and gave Patty's hand a squeeze.

Patty stared at him in disbelief. "I've never done *Guys and Dolls* before!" she gasped. "And I only had two days to look over the script and songs!"

"Relax, Patty. Don't worry! I told Ned you did the show a few years ago, so you'd need a little brushing up. Just smile a lot and fake it," he said as they pulled up in front of the theater.

George helped Patty out of the car. She saw a group of people walking toward them. Her knees felt as if they were about to give out.

George put his arm on her shoulder. "Patty," he said, "I'd like you to meet Ned Laramie. Ned, this is Patty Newton."

Patty shook hands with the short, curly-haired director. "Welcome to the cast," Ned said with a smile. "George has told us a lot about you."

"It was all good," George added with a wink.

Ned's smile suddenly faded. "Opening night is only ten days away. We have no time to lose. So we'll begin as soon as you get into your dance clothes. When we break for dinner, George will show

"Welcome to the cast," Ned said with a smile.

you your room."

Ned Laramie certainly doesn't waste any time, Patty thought.

As she changed into her leotard and tights, Patty thought about her role. She played the part of Mimi, who only had a few lines. She had a lot of singing and dancing, but it was usually with a group. Patty would have to follow along as best she could.

One of the actresses entered the dressing room. "Ned wants to know if you're ready," she said. "By the way, my name is Toni. Welcome aboard."

"Thanks," Patty said. She fastened the strap on her dancing shoe. "O.K., I'm ready."

"Listen, Patty, don't let Ned scare you," Toni said. "His bark is worse than his bite."

Toni led Patty out to the stage and introduced her to the rest of the cast.

"All right, everyone. Let's get started! We'll take it from the top. Your opening poses, please!" Ned said. "Patty, stand center stage, facing right. As the curtain opens, you're powdering your nose. Make eyes at the guys over there. Walk very slowly past George and exit. Places!"

The pianist began to play. Patty powdered her nose. As she walked toward George, Ned yelled, "Cut! Patty, try to be a bit more lively. You're trying to catch his eye, remember?" Ned was pointing at George.

Patty blushed and took her place again. She was sure Ned knew she had never done the show before. Well, she'd show him! This time, she swayed her hips, rolled her eyes, and sighed as she walked by George.

Ned laughed out loud. "Perfect! That was just right, Patty. Let's not forget this is a very funny show, kids! Let yourself go! Toni, would you work with Patty during the guys' next scene? Go over the girls' numbers."

As Toni led Patty off-stage, Patty gave George a wink. Things were going to be all right, after all.

Leading Man

Rehearsal ended at seven. Patty was very tired. She'd been singing and dancing for six hours. Her head was spinning from trying to learn so much at once. Rehearsals had started two weeks before she'd arrived. Now she had a lot of catching up to do. Opening night was only ten days away!

Patty sank into a front-row seat. She

sighed. George came over and kissed her on the cheek.

"You're a real pro, jumping into the show the way you did," he said. "You'll learn the part in no time. I promise tomorrow will be easier. The first day is always the worst," George said. "Are you ready for some good country cooking?"

"That sounds great! I'm as hungry as a bear!" Patty exclaimed. "I was too nervous to eat any lunch."

"Good, I know just the spot! There's a nice little place down the road with great food. What do you say?"

"I'll be ready in five minutes!" Patty was in the dressing room before George could say a word.

The other actresses were also changing into their street clothes. Toni Carmine smiled at Patty.

Patty sank into a front-row seat.

"You did a great job today," Toni said warmly.

"Gee, thanks," Patty said.

"Listen," said Toni. "If you have any questions about the show, just ask. I'm in Room 21."

"Thanks, I may take you up on that," Patty smiled. Toni had been so warm and friendly all day. Patty hoped that the two of them could become friends.

"Patty," George called from outside. "Are you almost ready? I'm starving!"

"I'll be right there, George!" Patty stuffed her dance clothes into her bag. She swung it over her shoulder. "See you later," she said to Toni.

"Have fun," Toni replied with a wink.

George and Patty walked out of the theater arm in arm. Patty was so happy! She felt like telling the whole world about it. Three days ago, she had been out of work and depressed. Now, thanks to George, she had a great summer job. The theater was far away from all city worries. The other actors seemed really nice. And, best of all, she got to dance with George every day. Patty had had a crush on George ever since they'd danced together last summer. He'd been involved with someone else then, but now...?

George drew her closer and put his arm around her. "I'm so glad you came up here."

"I am, too," Patty said softly. She smiled up into George's sparkling eyes. The couple walked on happily along a tree-lined street.

"Oh, what a lovely house!" Patty pointed to a small, cozy cottage.

"I thought you'd like it. That's Hanover House, the restaurant I was telling you about. It used to be a private home."

Hanover House was the most romantic place Patty had ever seen. Hundreds of flowers lined the path to the door. The trees next to the restaurant sparkled with tiny, darting lights.

"Those are fireflies," George explained.

"I've never seen so many at once!" Patty gasped. "They're beautiful."

The inside of Hanover House was even more romantic. There were fresh flowers on every table. Patty and George were seated in a quiet corner. Candles were the only light.

George took Patty's hand and looked into her eyes. Before he could speak, a voice called out, "George! What a big

Hanover House was the most romantic place Patty had ever seen.

surprise running into you here!"

Eddie Young, the leading man in the show, walked over to their table. "I hope you don't mind if I join you," he said. He pulled up a chair. "I've been dying to meet our new dancer."

George glared at Eddie as he introduced Patty.

"I'm delighted to meet you," Eddie said. He kissed Patty's hand. She giggled and George frowned.

"Where's Jody tonight?" George asked Eddie. "Have you two had a fight?"

"Jody? Oh, she's supposed to meet me here," Eddie replied. "I guess she's late, as usual. Patty, dear, I thought you were wonderful today. You charmed our grouchy director just like that." He snapped his fingers. "And, I might add, you charmed someone else as well."

Patty looked down at the tablecloth. Eddie sure knew how to pour it on thick. But she had to admit she was flattered. He was very good-looking.

"You just can't resist, can you?" George muttered under his breath. His comment was for Eddie's ears. But Patty heard it, too. It made her angry. *Does George think he owns me?* she thought.

Patty turned to Eddie with her brightest smile. "I'm grateful to you and the others for making me feel at home here," she said sweetly. "I'm really looking forward to working on this show."

"I'm looking forward to working with *you*," Eddie said. He pulled his chair closer to Patty. Just then, Jody Adams stormed over to Eddie.

"How dare you leave me at the theater

37

"I'm looking forward to working with you,"
Eddie said.

like that! You didn't even bother to tell me where you were going! You'd better have a good story!" she roared.

"For Pete's sake, Jody. Stop making a scene," Eddie muttered. "I can explain everything." He quickly excused himself and left with Jody. She was still yelling at him as the door closed behind them.

George and Patty looked at each other. They burst out laughing.

"I think they were made for each other," Patty said. "What a pair they make!"

"You didn't seem to think Eddie was so funny a few minutes ago." George was frowning again. He was really jealous of Eddie Young!

"Are you suggesting that I talk to no one but you?" Patty teased.

"Well," George was smiling now, "I wouldn't mind that. But you'd get awfully bored." He looked more serious as he took Patty's hand. "I'm sorry if I was out of line just now. Can you forgive me?"

"Sure, George, if you promise me one thing."

"What's that, Patty?"

"Promise me you won't think about Eddie anymore tonight. I know I won't."

"It's a deal," George said with a grin. "Now where were we before we were so rudely interrupted…?"

Teamwork

Patty sat at the piano in the empty studio. She played the same notes over and over. She sang the tune softly. But something wasn't right. This number was important. The whole cast was in it, with Burton Sachs singing the lead. The harmonies were confusing. Yesterday, Ned had yelled at Patty for mixing up her part with someone else's.

Patty leaned her head on her hand and sighed. *I wish I'd had more voice lessons*, she thought miserably. The dancing in the show was no problem. In fact, it was a lot of fun. But some of the singing worried her.

"Hey, Patty, are you O.K.?" Toni asked.

Patty was startled. She hadn't heard Toni come in.

Toni sat down next to Patty on the piano bench. "Patty, I heard you working on those harmonies. You almost had it, but you forgot the B-flat. Do you mind if I show you?"

"Please do. I need all the help I can get with this song!" said Patty.

Toni sang the tune as she played. When she explained the song, it all seemed so easy. Within five minutes,

"Hey, Patty, are you O.K.?" Toni asked.

Patty could sing the notes correctly. It still needed some work, but the song sounded so much better!

When Ned walked in, Patty and Toni stood up. It was time to get ready for rehearsal.

"Toni, how can I ever thank you? I've learned more in five minutes with you than I have in the last three days practicing on my own. Have you ever taught voice lessons?"

"No, not really. I just help friends out sometimes," Toni said.

"You should think about teaching. You're a natural!"

"Well, I don't know about that. But I'm glad I could help you. Maybe we'll work on the song again later. There's no time to lose with opening night only a week away!"

"Oh, don't remind me," Patty groaned. "Listen, Toni, I'd love for you to coach me on the music. But I want to do something for you, too. How would you like to start dance classes?"

"You know I'd like to, but where?" said Toni. "There's no dance teacher for miles around here."

"You're looking at her," Patty said. "How would you like to swap dance lessons for voice lessons? We could coach each other on the dances and songs in the show."

"You know, that's a great idea!" Toni said with a grin. "I could really use some help on those dances."

"And I need help on the songs!" said Patty.

"When do we start?" Toni asked.

"How about tomorrow morning?"

"Great!" The girls were still talking when Ned cleared his throat.

"Everybody on stage!" Ned shouted. Toni and Patty hurried to their places for the next scene.

The next morning at ten, they met in Patty's room.

"Boy, am I sleepy," Toni said with a yawn.

"Me, too," Patty said. "Ned's really working us to the limit these days. What time did we stop last night—midnight?"

"At least," Toni replied. "All I know is it was two-thirty in the morning when I got home."

"Did you go out with Burton last night?" Patty asked.

"Mmm-hmm," Toni said dreamily. "We went to that little café in town. It

"Everybody on stage!" Ned shouted.

was very cozy and we had a great talk, but..." Toni sighed.

"Is he still treating you like one of the guys?" Patty asked.

"Yes," Toni admitted.

"Well, I've got a plan to make Burton notice you."

Toni saw the twinkle in Patty's eye. "What is it, Patty? I can tell you've got something up your sleeve."

Patty grinned. "After we finish your dance class, we'll get you all fixed up. Today you'll leave your T-shirt and sweat pants at home. Instead, you'll wear my red leotard. With some make-up and a new hairdo, he'll really notice you."

"I don't know, Patty. How can I go to rehearsal like that? People will stare at me."

"*Burton* will stare at you. That's the

whole idea, Toni!"

"We'll see. First, let's get down to work," Toni said firmly.

The girls began the dance class with some stretching exercises on the floor.

"Oh, am I out of shape!" Toni groaned. Slowly, she warmed up her legs and back. Then she stood up and did arm circles and toe touches.

"Very good. You're doing fine," Patty said. "Just don't push too hard on the first day." She had Toni hold on to a chair and gave her some ballet steps to do. "Don't forget to breathe," Patty joked when Toni looked tense. Class ended with big leg swings and jumps.

"I think that's enough for today," Patty said.

"Thanks. That was a good workout," Toni replied. "How about if we do your

49

voice lesson at three? I think the piano is free then."

"That's fine. Now what about that red leotard?"

Toni decided to go along with Patty's plan after all. She put on Patty's silky, red leotard. Then Patty braided colored beads into Toni's hair.

"You look great!" she told Toni.

Toni stared at herself in the bathroom mirror. "I hardly recognize myself! I'll be so happy if Burton looks at me the way George looks at you."

Patty blushed. "What do you mean?"

"I mean he adores you."

"Well, I'm sure head-over-heels for him! I think about him all the time. And when we dance—I'm in heaven! Do you really think he likes me?"

"I *know* so. I'm surprised he hasn't

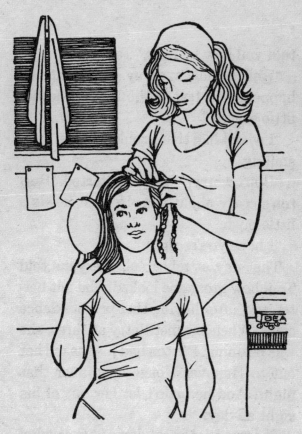

Patty braided colored beads into Toni's hair.

told you how he feels," Toni said.

"Well, he has, in a way. I mean, it's all happened so fast, I think we're both a little scared."

"I wish I had that problem," Toni said, smiling.

"Don't worry," Patty comforted. "Burton's crazy about you. He just needs a little push."

"I hope you're right."

That day at rehearsal, everyone told Toni how great she looked. She felt better, too, after having that private dance class. When she met Patty at three, she was beaming. Burton had just asked her out to Hanover House for dinner that night. And he hadn't let her out of his sight all day.

The two friends sat down at the piano. Toni gave Patty voice warm-ups. She helped her with her breathing and timing on songs. Patty picked it all up quickly. She sounded much better already.

"Thanks, Toni. That really helped!" Patty said with a smile.

Toni smiled back. "We're going to be a great team!"

Better Late Than Never

Ned scowled and looked at his watch. Rehearsal was called for five o'clock and it was already ten after. Where was the pianist?

"Has anyone seen David?" Ned asked the cast.

"He said he was going into Glendale to put up some posters," Toni said.

"Has anyone seen David?" Ned asked the cast.

"I know that!" Ned barked. "I let him take my car. But where is he? It's only a ten-minute ride to Glendale."

Toni gave Ned a hurt look and walked to the other side of the stage to stretch. He sure was touchy today. It was going to be a long rehearsal.

"Maybe he got stuck behind a slow-moving tractor," Burton suggested.

"Or a cow in the middle of the road," George added. "But, more likely, he met a girl and fell in love." George clutched his heart and rolled his eyes.

"Yes, he's overdue. How long has it been since his last love ended? Three or four days?" Burton laughed and elbowed George. Ned gave them both a dirty look and started pacing back and forth in front of the stage.

"Oh, brother. I can see we're in for it

tonight," Patty whispered to Toni.

"You can say that again. I feel a storm brewing," Toni said. "I hope David gets here soon — for his sake and ours."

The cast was scattered throughout the theater. Two dancers warmed up downstage. The leading man stood in the middle of the stage rehearsing some lines. Several singers practiced harmonies in the corner. The rest of the cast stood in groups of two or three, talking and laughing.

Ned's pacing became more frantic as the minutes passed. It was twenty past five. Ned smiled darkly as he planned what he would say to David. He came up with three separate speeches before he settled on the right words. How dare he come so late with only two more rehearsals before opening night?

"Psst, Patty!" Toni called her friend over. "He's starting to talk to himself. That's Stage Two." She gestured toward Ned.

"What was Stage One?" Patty asked.

"Pacing," Toni replied. "Stage Three is pulling his hair. And Stage Four is throwing a fit."

Ned's muttering was getting louder. "Why didn't I become a farmer—or a gardener? I like flowers. They like me. They don't talk back. They don't go into Glendale and disappear. Why didn't I listen to my mother?" Ned raised his voice an octave. "'Ned, my son, an actor's life is no life at all. Why don't you go into business, like your father?'" He groaned and started pulling at his hair.

Toni looked at Patty and they giggled. "What did I tell you?"

"You know, he's pretty funny," Patty said. "Are you sure he didn't start as a stand-up comic?"

"I wouldn't be surprised if he did," Toni said. "He doesn't talk much about himself. But I hear he was quite an actor before he went into directing."

Ned stopped pacing and faced the cast with a determined look. "Quiet, everyone! Let me have your attention!" The cast fell silent, and Ned went on.

"We have just wasted half an hour waiting for David. You've all worked far too hard to let one person ruin this show. With or without David, the show must go on. There are only two days till opening night. We haven't a minute to lose. We're taking the show from the top. Places, everyone!"

The cast members took their places

silently. They looked grim. The show was going to be very hard to do without any music. Almost every scene had a song or dance number.

Ned raised his right hand. "Ready and one...two...three...four." He kept the rhythm by snapping his fingers and tapping his foot. "Cut!" he yelled after a few moments. "Who died?" he asked with a frown. "You all look as if you're at a funeral. I wouldn't pay a nickel to see a show like that! People come to the theater to be entertained, not bored to tears! Take it from the top again."

The actors shuffled to their places and Ned raised his right hand. Just then, a car honked loudly outside the theater. There was a grinding, bumpety-bump sound and then a screech of brakes.

Ned rushed outside, followed by the

cast. His mouth dropped open as David got out of the car, which was leaning to one side. The right front tire was in shreds and David was covered with grease.

"My car!" Ned groaned.

"I'm touched to see your concern for me," David said to Ned. The cast members were all asking him questions at once.

"Quiet, everybody! Let him speak!" Ned yelled over the noise. He turned to David. "Tell us what happened."

"I got a flat tire about halfway back from Glendale. I tried to change the tire, but your spare was flat. I waited awhile, hoping someone would come by. There wasn't a car on the road. So I drove her home myself, taking it real easy." David looked Ned in the eye. "You owe me a

"My car!" Ned groaned.

new shirt, Ned. I got an oil shower when I tried to change that tire. That car needs a lot of work."

Ned felt guilty about all the nasty things he had planned to say to David. "I'm sorry about the spare. I've been meaning to patch it up for months. I'll throw in a free dinner at Hanover House along with the new shirt. It's the least I can do. But first..." Ned paused.

"I know," David laughed, looking at Ned's worried face. "The show must go on. Just let me get washed up and we can get started."

"Thanks, David. You're a real pro!" Ned said warmly. "Take five, everyone!"

A Little Romance

"Take five, everyone! Then we'll start with the dream ballet."

The stage cleared at once. The cast hadn't had a break in two hours. Patty ducked into the dressing room to freshen up. The dream ballet was her big number with George. It was her favorite scene.

But one part scared Patty. Toward the end of the dance, she ran across the stage toward George. Then she leaped into his arms and he swung her high in the air. Their timing had to be perfect for the lift to work. And they only had three more rehearsals to get it right.

"Places, everyone!" Ned shouted.

Patty hurried out of the dressing room. The music began just as she got backstage. She took a deep breath and waited for her cue.

Patty made her entrance and the music washed over her. Her fear slipped away as she began her slow, dreamy dance.

George entered from the other side of the stage. He glided over to her and held out his hand. Would she dance with him?

At first, she turned away shyly. But when she looked back, he knew the answer was yes. He took her hand and drew her close. She slipped her arm around his neck and let him take her weight. He lifted her gently. She seemed to walk on air. As her feet touched the ground, she broke away, but only for a moment.

Patty lifted her right leg high behind her. She rose up on her left foot and arched her back. With a toss of her head, she seemed to dive toward the floor. She really let herself go this time. When George swept her in his arms, a gasp went through the theater.

Patty totally trusted George now. They were moving and breathing as one person. Their timing was perfect! Patty had never felt so free and joyful. She

George took Patty's hand and drew her close.

danced each step as if she'd been born to do it.

George had never lifted her so high. And his own dancing was smooth as velvet. When their eyes met, Patty knew George wasn't just acting. This love duet was for real.

The whole cast of the show watched the dancers. No one spoke a word. A sense of magic seemed to fill the theater.

The music reached its dramatic peak. Patty ran toward George and leaped into his arms. She hit a perfect split as he swung her high in an arch. He set her down and they embraced.

The music faded. They walked offstage very slowly, arm in arm.

There was a moment of silence. Then the other actors burst into applause. Even Ned, the director, was whistling and cheering wildly.

"That was wonderful!" Ned exclaimed. He jumped to his feet. "Come out here, you two!"

Patty and George were still in the wings. They couldn't face the others just yet. It would break the spell.

They were both breathing too hard to say much. But it didn't matter. Their looks said it all.

Patty brushed a strand of hair out of George's eyes. Sweaty as they were, George bent over and kissed Patty.

"You were incredible!" he said softly.

"So were you!" Patty whispered.

"Would you kids get out here? We've got a whole show to rehearse!" Ned shouted.

Patty sighed. "Come on," she said, taking George's hand. "I don't want to get us in trouble."

As the two dancers appeared on stage, they had to face some teasing. But Ned ended that quickly. "All right, everyone. That's enough." Then to Patty and George he said, "Take a breather, you two. I don't need you for the next scene."

George and Patty got their dance bags and sat down in the back of the theater. George wiped his dripping face with a towel. He left it wrapped around his neck like a scarf.

"Whew! I think I sweat more after I stop dancing!" he said.

"I know what you mean." Patty wiped her own damp brow and sank back in the chair.

"Patty, we were making magic out there!" George said. "I've never danced

"Patty, we were making magic out there!"
George said.

as well with anyone else."

"Neither have I." Patty rested her head on his shoulder.

George held her close. "What do you say we celebrate tonight? Burton told me about a nightclub in Glen Cove. They have a live band and dancing starts at ten."

"That sounds great! But can we borrow a car?"

"Well, Ned needs his car. But I think we can borrow Burton's car. He and Toni aren't doing anything tonight."

"Listen, everyone!" Ned shouted. "I just heard from the costume designer. The only time she can make it is at nine o'clock tomorrow morning. So your call is for 8:45. Don't be late! Patty, I'll need you to stay late tonight. I'm adding a new section to one of your dances."

Patty looked at George and sighed. "So much for our night out," she said.

"We'll just have to make it another time," George said with a smile.

"Places!" Ned shouted. "We're taking it from the top."

"Oh, brother!" Patty said. "I thought we were almost done!"

"I should have warned you. Ned goes crazy the last couple of days before a show opens." George helped Patty to her feet.

"Well, that's show biz!" Patty gave him a tired smile in return.

"That's the spirit," said George. "We'll get through this together."

Down to the Wire

Patty was getting excited. The show opened tomorrow! She couldn't believe she'd been in Riverdale for ten days. It seemed as if she'd just arrived! Yet so much had happened. There had been a lot of hard work, but she didn't mind. She loved the theater!

Then there was her romance with George. That made the last ten days even more wonderful. And she'd become great friends with Toni. In fact, she felt close to the whole group. It was funny how quickly actors got to know each other. Toni probably knew more about Patty than some of her old friends did!

By the time Patty reached the theater, some of the other actors were already warming up. The stage crew was hanging lights. Ned was sorting through a pile of costumes.

Patty greeted everyone. Then she headed for the dressing room.

"Hi, Patty!" Toni said. She was changing into sweat pants and a T-shirt.

"Hi, Toni!" Patty set down her dance bag. She began laying out her things. "I came well prepared today," she added,

The stage crew was hanging lights.

taking out a bag of cookies. "Do you want one?"

"No, thanks. I just had a big breakfast. I'll see you out there." Toni picked up her bag and went to warm up.

Patty changed into her dance clothes and went out on stage. Blue and red lights flashed on and off. A spotlight caught her face and swept past her. The lighting crew was hard at work. Today, they were setting the lights for the show.

Patty lay down on the stage and began stretching.

"Oh, Patty, would you come here for a minute?" Ned yelled. He was holding a green satin dress. "I want you to try this on," he told her.

Patty slipped the dress on right over her dance clothes.

"No, no, no!" Ned said with a wave of his hand. "It's all wrong! I should have done the costumes myself. Take it off."

Patty gave the dress back to him.

"Here, try this," he said. He handed her a sky-blue dress trimmed with lace.

"That's beautiful!" Patty exclaimed. She had to have this costume. It fit her like a dream. The top of the dress was soft and clingy. At the hips, it flared out in graceful folds. Patty spun around, making the skirt fly.

"I love it!" she told Ned.

"It's yours," he said with a smile.

"Oh, thank you! Do you mind if I show George?"

"No, go ahead. Just don't get it dirty."

Patty ran over to the door of the men's dressing room. "George, come out here for a second! It's Patty. I have a

Patty spun around, making the skirt fly.

surprise for you!"

George appeared a second later, barefoot and without a shirt. "What on earth is so—" He stopped dead in his tracks when he saw Patty. "Wow!" he said with a low whistle. "You look gorgeous!"

"Do you like my surprise?" she asked. She felt like a princess.

"I love it! Is that for our number?" George asked. He couldn't take his eyes off her.

"Don't touch her!" Ned growled.

"O.K., Ned, take it easy," George said with a laugh.

Patty slipped off the dress and returned it to Ned.

"You'd better change your clothes," Ned told George. "We're starting in five minutes."

"Do you see all the trouble you get me

into?" George teased Patty. He ducked into the dressing room before she could reply.

Lighting the show took five hours. Each new scene required a change in the lights. Changes in mood required red or blue or green lights. Sometimes the lighting person had to follow an actor with a spotlight. Scenes were repeated over and over until the lights were right. With all the stops and starts, it was soon five o'clock.

"Listen, kids, you have a choice," Ned began. "We can take a dinner break and start the dress rehearsal at eight. Or we can take a short break and begin it right away. All in favor of starting at eight, raise your hands."

No one raised a hand.

"Then we'll start as soon as you're all

ready," Ned said. "Anyone who still has costume problems, see me."

George went to a nearby diner to get coffee for everyone.

Back in the dressing room, Patty and Toni dug into the cookies.

"Hey, I just remembered I have some apples in my bag," Toni said suddenly. "Would you like some?"

"Yes, let's eat something healthy for a change," Patty said.

It wasn't long before George returned. "Hey, ladies! The coffee express is back!"

While they all sat around drinking coffee, Ned talked to the cast. "I want to start in fifteen minutes. We're going to run straight through the show. We won't stop unless there's a disaster. I want you to do it as if this were a real performance. If you get sloppy in rehearsals, you'll be sloppy in performances. That's all."

The dress rehearsal went pretty smoothly. There were only two stops. The first was when George stumbled doing a jump. The second was when Burton missed an entrance.

After they finished, Ned spoke about some little problems with this or that scene. "But I think you did a really good job," he said proudly. "Now I don't know about you, but I'm starving! Who'd like to join me for some pizza? It's my treat."

"I will!"

"Me, too!"

"Count me in!"

Soon the whole cast had decided to go.

"Burton, can we squeeze some hungry people into your car? My car only holds eight," Ned said.

"Sure thing! I can take the rest."

"Good! Then we're all set. Just let me call Joe's Pizzeria and tell them to expect a crowd!"

Opening Night

Patty sat down in front of the dressing-room mirror. It was seven-fifteen, time to put on her make-up. Curtain time was eight o'clock. She took a deep breath and let it out slowly. Her heart was racing. She had to calm down.

Toni rushed into the dressing room. "Patty, do you have a needle and thread? My hem's coming down."

"What color thread do you need?" Patty asked.

"Something light. Do you have beige?"

Patty pulled a sewing kit out of her bag. "Let's see now...Here's some tan thread. How's that?"

"That's fine," Toni replied. Her hand shook as she threaded the needle. "Boy, am I nervous!" she said.

"You and me both!" laughed Patty.

"Did you hear about the light?" Toni asked. "They can't fix it. Ned says we can cover with the other lights. I hope he's right."

"We'll just have to make the best of it," Patty said. "It wouldn't feel like opening night if *something* wasn't wrong." She laughed nervously.

"I know what you mean," Toni said. She finished her sewing. "I'll see you later. I've got to find the iron. This costume wrinkles if I look at it!"

"Take it easy!" Patty called after her.

She pulled her hair off her face with a headband. Then she put on the first layer of make-up. Over that came powder and rouge. Now for the eyes. Patty brushed white eye shadow under her eyebrows. She shaded the crease above her eyes with brown. A touch of green on the eyelids accented her green eyes.

Patty calmed down as she applied her make-up. It helped her get in the mood for the show.

She followed the line of her eyes with brown eyeliner. False eyelashes and lipstick were the final touches. Patty smiled at herself in the mirror. She liked what she saw.

"Fifteen minutes!" Ned yelled through the door. It was time to get in costume. All the actresses were in the tiny dressing room now. Some were very quiet. Others whispered nervously.

Patty slipped on her costume for the opening number. Toni zipped her up, then Patty fixed Toni's hair.

"Five minutes!" Ned yelled.

The dressing room buzzed with conversation. Toni sang softly. Patty fastened her dance shoes. She had to see George before the show.

Patty found George on the stage. He was going through some steps.

"Oh, George, I had to see you!" Patty was breathless with excitement.

"Hi, Patty! I thought you'd never

Patty smiled at herself in the mirror.

come out of there," George teased. "How about a kiss for good luck?"

"If you promise not to smear my make-up!"

George held Patty close. She could feel his heart racing. He was nervous, too, though he'd never admit it.

"We're going to be great tonight! I can just *feel* it," Patty exclaimed.

"I hope your feelings are right," George said.

"On stage! Places, everyone!" Ned shouted.

The actors hurried to their places. The music began. The curtain opened. They were on!

The opening number went smoothly. The cast seemed to glow with energy. Everyone's nervousness faded away. The audience was great, too. People clapped loudly. They laughed out loud during the funny scenes.

The show was flying by! Before long, it was time for Patty's big number with George. Her heart pounded as she waited in the wings. What if she forgot a step? What if their timing was off? What if she slipped? Suddenly, she was all nerves again.

The music began. Patty could see George standing in the wings across from her. He blew her a kiss.

When she made her entrance, the dance took over. She left nervous Patty Newton somewhere in the wings. Her dancing was smooth and flowing.

George entered and offered her his hand. She smiled at him. Soon she was floating high above the stage in his arms. He set her down gently. They

George blew Patty a kiss.

parted for a moment.

The music got faster and faster. George and Patty whirled across the stage. Again they parted. Patty paused at the edge of the stage. George reached toward her from the other side. She ran toward him and leaped into his arms. As he swept her high in the air, the audience gasped. She seemed to be flying!

George lowered her against his chest. He turned with her in his arms. The music began to fade as he set her down. The lights dimmed as the couple walked off-stage, arm in arm.

The audience burst into wild applause.

Patty and George hugged each other in the wings.

"We did it!" Patty whispered.

"We were great!" said George.

"See you later. I've got to change for the finale!" Patty hurried toward the dressing room.

Patty dabbed herself with a towel. She tried to unzip her dress but it got stuck.

"Oh, no!" she moaned. There was no one in the dressing room to help her. She ran backstage and grabbed Toni.

"Help me, quick!" she whispered. "My zipper's stuck!"

Toni fiddled with the zipper. It wouldn't budge. Finally, she gave it a really hard yank. Patty almost fell over.

"There! It's unzipped!" Toni whispered. "You'd better hurry!"

Patty flew back to the dressing room. She threw her dress off. The music for the finale was starting! She flung her

The cast took five curtain calls.

costume over her head and ran out. Patty got to her place just in time.

The finale went beautifully. The cast took five curtain calls. The show was a big success!

As soon as the curtain closed, the cast went wild. They jumped up and down, hugging and kissing each other. There was nothing like opening night!